Celestine

Drama Queen

Celestine

Drama Queen

Even before Celestine had hatched from her egg,
the Duck family knew there was
someone very special inside.

"Tappity tap, tappity tap," went the egg each day until –

crack!

– out danced Celestine, ready to be a star.

Right from the start,
Celestine was very hard to ignore.

As soon as she was old enough, Celestine would dress herself with great care, just as a real star should.

Sometimes it took
rather a long time
to create **just** the right look.

"Do you think you should be wearing a tiara to school, Celestine?" her mother asked.

"Of course! A star must set an example," said Celestine, skipping out of the door.

At school, Miss MacDonald called the register.

"Archie?"

"Yes, Miss MacDonald."

"Beattie?"

"Yes, Miss MacDonald."

"Celestine?"

"Celestine's not here,"
answered Celestine.
"Today you may call me

Princess Druscilla Drake -
it's a much better name for a star, don't you think?"

"Well, Princess Druscilla Drake," said her teacher, "this morning we all have the chance to be someone else – we are going to begin rehearsals for our school play."

"I would be delighted to accept the lead role," beamed Celestine, twirling round the room.

"Thank you, Celestine," said Miss MacDonald. "There's an important part for everyone."

On the way home that afternoon, Celestine sighed,
"Stars don't walk, they should ride. Especially when
they've got the best part in a new play."

"And what IS your part?" asked her brother.

"That's a secret," smiled Celestine,
        tap dancing along the pavement.

After tea, Celestine rushed straight up to her room.
"I have to rehearse for the play now, Mummy," she
shouted, slamming her bedroom door shut.

"Shall I hear your lines, Celestine?" called her mother through the door a little later.

"No, thank you," Celestine called back cheerfully. "They're very nearly perfect."

"Shall I help you practise?" asked her brother the following day.
"No, thank you," said Celestine,
"I know
every
word!"

The day of the play came at last. Celestine breezed jauntily into her classroom blowing kisses into the air.

"How kind," she thought, noticing some flowers nearby. "Someone has sent me a bouquet!"

"But where is my red carpet?"
she wondered, walking down
to the hall.

"And the rest of the orchestra's late!"
she frowned, seeing only Mrs Gobble
at her keyboard.

The moment had arrived.
All the little chicks and ducks huddled backstage.
The lights dimmed.
The audience grew quiet,
and the show began!

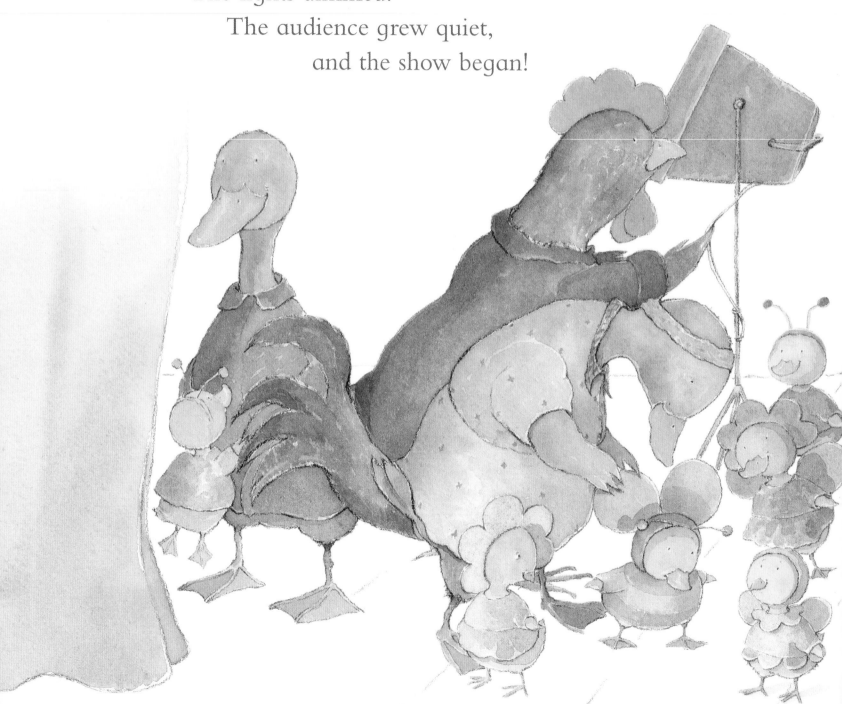

Celestine watched, trembling, behind the side
curtains, whispering along with every word.
"Time for you to go on now, dear,"
smiled Miss MacDonald.

But suddenly, Celestine's feet wouldn't work.
She was terrified!
"I feel **sick**," she coughed weakly.

"I'm going
to faint,"
she gasped.

"I won't!
I shan't!
I...I can't!"

she squeaked.

Miss MacDonald gently pushed her forward.
Celestine inched to the centre of the stage,
her heart beating madly –

pitter-pat,   pitter-pat.

She blinked at the bright lights;
she opened her beak...

but nothing came out!

Celestine stood
quite still –
she couldn't
move a feather.

"THE END!"

whispered
Miss MacDonald
from behind the curtain.

"Celestine, say your line!
Say 'THE END'!"

Then Mrs Gobble flew to her rescue, striking up one last, fast, jazzy tune on the piano.

Quite of their own accord, Celestine's feet began to tap,

her knees bent

and soon she was, with one final leap… until, with one final leap… whirling and turning, skipping and spinning,

The audience **loved** it!

"Well done!" they cheered,
clapping and clapping.

They all agreed it was a splendid
end to a wonderful show.

"Hurrah!"

"Brilliant!"

"Superb!"

But walking home, Celestine
was unusually quiet and thoughtful.

Flip-flop, flip-flop
flapped her little feet.

"I'm still a star, aren't I, Mummy?
Even though I forgot my line?" she asked at bedtime,
a big tear dripping down her beak.

"Of course you are, my darling!" said Mrs Duck,
buttoning up Celestine's pyjamas.
"Just think of that marvellous dance you did!
And besides..."

"...you'll **always** be a star to me!"
and she gave Celestine a kiss.

"Good night, little star,
good night."

A TEMPLAR BOOK

First published in the UK in 2008 by Templar Publishing
This edition published in 2014 by Templar Publishing,
an imprint of The Templar Company Limited,
Deepdene Lodge, Deepdene Avenue, Dorking, Surrey, RH5 4AT, UK
www.templarco.co.uk

1 3 5 7 9 10 8 6 2

ISBN 978-1-78370-098-1

Designed by Caroline Reeves
Edited by Stella Gurney

Printed in China